Pebble® Plus

Construction Zone

Digging Tunnels

by JoAnn Early Macken

Consulting Editor: Gail Saunders-Smith, PhD

Consultant: Don Matson, owner
Metro Construction, Paving, and Excavating
Roseville, Minnesota

Capstone
press®

Mankato, Minnesota

Pebble Plus is published by Capstone Press,
151 Good Counsel Drive, P.O. Box 669, Mankato, Minnesota 56002.
www.capstonepress.com

1 2 3 4 5 6 13 12 11 10 09 08

Library of Congress Cataloging-in-Publication Data
Macken, JoAnn Early, 1953–
   Digging tunnels/by JoAnn Early Macken.
   p. cm. — (Pebble plus. Construction zone)
   Summary: "Simple text and photographs present the digging of a tunnel, including information on the
workers and equipment needed" — Provided by publisher.
   Includes bibliographical references and index.
   ISBN-13: 978-1-4296-1234-0 (hardcover)
   ISBN-10: 1-4296-1234-7 (hardcover)
   1. Tunneling — Juvenile literature. 2. Tunnels — Juvenile literature. I. Title. II. Series.
TA807.M33 2008
624.1'93 — dc22   2007027107

Editorial Credits
Sarah L. Schuette, editor; Patrick Dentinger, designer; Jo Miller, photo researcher

Photo Credits
Alamy/allOver photography, cover; Andrew McCandlish, 11; Axel Hess, 1; Greenshoots Communications, 9;
   Roger Bamber, 19
Dreamstime/Pryzmat, 15
Getty Images Inc./David McNew, 13
iStockphoto/Kenneth C. Zirkel, 21
Shutterstock/Joanne Harris and Daniel Bubnich, 17; prism_68, 5
Visuals Unlimited/Pegasus, 7

Note to Parents and Teachers

The Construction Zone set supports national science standards related to understanding science and technology. This book describes and illustrates digging tunnels. The images support early readers in understanding the text. The repetition of words and phrases helps early readers learn new words. This book also introduces early readers to subject-specific vocabulary words, which are defined in the Glossary section. Early readers may need assistance to read some words and to use the Table of Contents, Glossary, Read More, Internet Sites, and Index sections of the book.

Table of Contents

Tunnels

Tunnels are underground
and underwater.
Cars, trains, and subways
move through tunnels.

Mines are tunnels too.

Miners dig for coal or gold

in these deep tunnels.

Making Plans

Many people work together
to build tunnels.
Engineers decide where
new tunnels are needed.

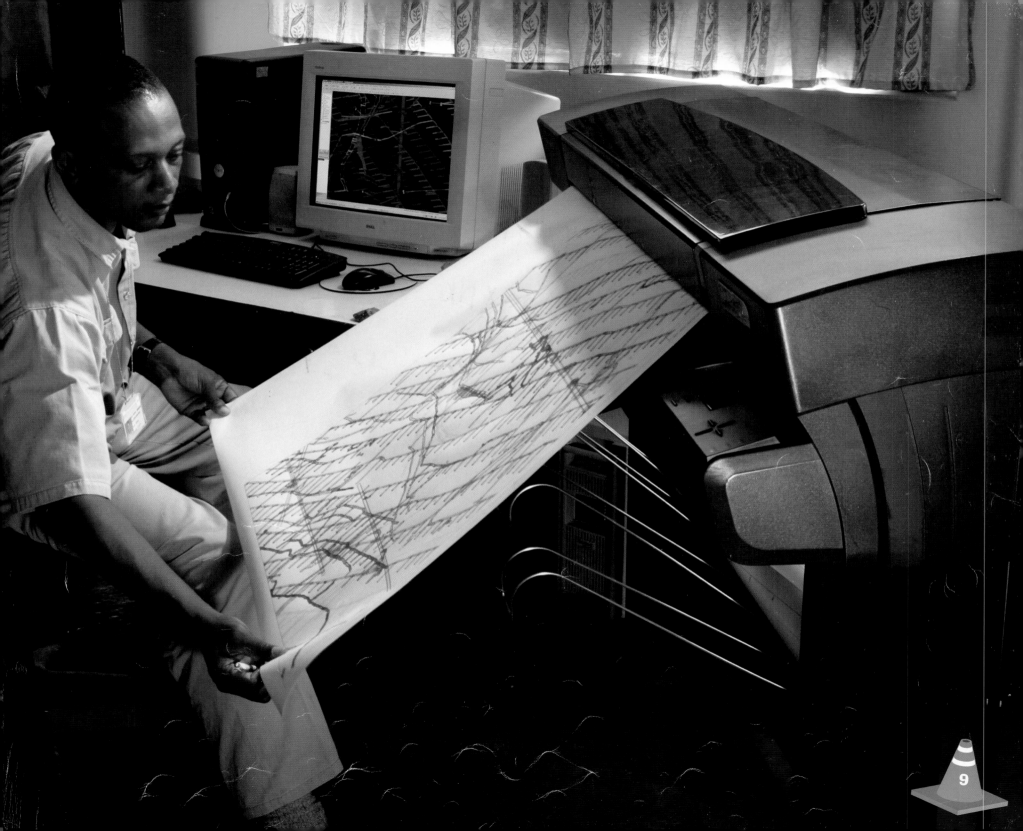

Geologists test
the soil and rock
in the area.
Then workers know what
machines to use.

Digging

Huge tunnel boring machines
drill through hard rock.
Sharp teeth break off pieces
of rock to make holes
in the ground.

Excavators dig deep trenches
in soft soil.
Workers put clay or concrete
on the sides to hold the soil
in place.

After digging the holes,
workers build walls
to line the tunnels.

Water pipes, gas pipes,

and power lines

are put in the tunnels.

Some tunnels stretch

for miles and miles.

New Tunnels

New tunnels open every day. People use them to get where they want to go.

21

Glossary

concrete — a mixture of cement, water, sand, and gravel that hardens as it dries

drill — to make a hole through something hard

engineer — a person who uses science to plan, design, or build

excavator — a machine with an arm and a bucket at the end that a driver can move

geologist — a person who studies the earth's layers of soil and rock

subway — a system of trains that runs underground in a city

trench — a long ditch or part of the ground that is dug out in a U shape

Read More

Mitchell, Susan K. *Longest Tunnels.* Megastructures. Milwaukee: Gareth Stevens, 2007.

Oxlade, Chris. *Tunnels.* Building Amazing Structures. Chicago: Heinemann, 2006.

Santella, Andrew. *Building the New York Subway.* Cornerstones of Freedom. New York: Children's Press, 2007.

Internet Sites

FactHound offers a safe, fun way to find Internet sites related to this book. All of the sites on FactHound have been researched by our staff.

Here's how:

1. Visit *www.facthound.com*

2. Choose your grade level.

3. Type in this book ID **1429612347** for age-appropriate sites. You may also browse subjects by clicking on letters, or by clicking on pictures and words.

4. Click on the **Fetch It** button.

FactHound will fetch the best sites for you!

Index

Word Count: 143
Grade: 1
Early-Intervention Level: 18